First published in the UK by HarperCollins Children's Books in 2008

HarperCollins Children's Books is a division of HarperCollins Publishers Ltd., 77-85 Fulham Palace Road, Hammersmith, London W6 8JB

ISBN 10: 0-00-728451-9
ISBN 13: 978-0-00-728451-1

www.narnia.com
www.discovernarnia.co.uk

A CIP catalogue record for this title is available from the British Library.

Printed and bound in Italy
by Rotolito Lombarda Spa

-THE CHRONICLES OF-
NARNIA
PRINCE CASPIAN

ANNUAL 2009

HarperCollins *Children's Books*

THE CHRONICLES OF
NARNIA
PRINCE CASPIAN

THE MOVIE

Adapted by Lana Jacobs
Based on the screenplay by Andrew Adamson &
Christopher Markus & Stephen McFeely
Based on the book by C. S. Lewis
Directed by Andrew Adamson

Professor Cornelius tiptoed into Prince Caspian's room in the middle of the night. He had to help his student escape the Telmarine soldiers who waited outside his door. Cornelius led Caspian out of the room through the secret passage in the wardrobe.

Just before Cornelius sent Caspian away from the castle on his horse, he handed Caspian a special gift. "Do not use it except at your greatest need. Everything you know is about to change," he said.

Upon discovering Caspian's room empty, the Telmarine soldiers searched the castle. Then they saw Caspian head towards the wood, so the soldiers followed him.

Suddenly, Caspian fell off his horse. He opened his eyes to find three creatures standing above him, two Dwarfs and a Badger. As they closed in on Caspian, he reached into the bag that contained Cornelius's gift . . . and pulled out an ivory horn. Caspian blew into the horn before the Dwarfs had a chance to stop him.

Nikabrik, one of the Dwarfs, knocked Caspian out with his sword. Nikabrik and his friends brought Caspian inside their den to find out more about that small white horn that Caspian carried with him.

Meanwhile, on a train platform in London, the Pevensie children struggled to adjust to ordinary lives filled with schoolbooks and uniforms. They fought with other children at school. They longed to return to their lives as Kings and Queens of Narnia.

"Remember what Aslan said: Once a King of Narnia, always a King of Narnia," Lucy reminded her siblings.

"I think it's time we accept that we live here. And now," Susan tried to reassure her family.

Just as Susan finished speaking, the children felt a strange sensation…

Moments later, the Pevensies found themselves standing on a white, sandy beach. Their dreams had come true . . . they were back in Narnia! But something in the distance looked unfamiliar. "I don't remember any ruins in Narnia," Edmund said.

Walking toward the ruins, Susan found a golden chess piece on the ground. Suddenly it dawned on Peter: They were standing before Cair Paravel, their former Narnian home.

Back at the castle, King Miraz and his advisors discussed the Prince's disappearance. By blaming everything on the Narnians, Miraz would be justified in starting a war that would allow him to claim the throne as his own. His plan came to life as his soldiers brought in a captured Narnian, a Dwarf.

"We forget that Narnia was once a savage land," Miraz reminded his council. "They've been watching us, waiting to strike — and I intend to strike back," he said as he pointed to the Dwarf.

Unaware of the trouble brewing, the children marvelled at the rubble that was once their glorious Cair Paravel. "This didn't just happen. Cair Paravel was attacked," Edmund declared.

They stumbled upon the treasure chamber, where Lucy found her cordial, Edmund his helmet, Peter his sword and shield and Susan her quiver and bow. The only thing missing was Susan's horn.

"I think it's time we found out what's going on," Peter declared.

Caspian awoke inside Trufflehunter the Badger's den. Caspian was shocked to hear Trufflehunter and Nikabrik speak . . . they were living Narnians, creatures from the fairy tales he had heard as a child!

As Caspian turned to leave, Nikabrik stopped him.

"You're meant to save us," Trufflehunter said, the ivory horn sitting nearby. "It is said that whoever sounds it will bring back the Ancient Kings and Queens . . . and lead us to freedom," the Badger explained.

Little did Caspian know that his magical horn had already brought back the Ancient Kings and Queens. Now dressed in Narnian garb, the children set out to learn exactly what had been going on while they were away. They were surprised to find Telmarine soldiers holding a Narnian captive. Susan immediately shot two arrows at the soldiers to save the Dwarf.

"Beards and bedsteads," Trumpkin exclaimed. These children were actually the Kings and Queens of old that he and the rest of the Narnians had been waiting for!

When Caspian met the rest of the Narnians on the Dancing Lawn, the crowd was angry, for they had learned to fear all Telmarines. By showing the horn, Caspian tried to convince them that he could bring peace to Narnia —if they would help him claim his throne from the evil Miraz.

The Narnians didn't believe Caspian's promise, but Trufflehunter quickly came to his aid: "We Badgers remember well that Narnia was never right except when a Son of Adam was King." The Narnians agreed: It was time for Caspian to take his place as King and restore order to the land of Narnia.

The Narnians weren't the only ones who longed for the Narnia of old. Lucy
was saddened to learn that the trees no longer danced and the Bears were no
longer her friends.

As the children crossed the river to enter the wood, Lucy saw something
spectacular. "Aslan!" she cried. But nobody saw the Great Lion except for Lucy.

Later that night, Lucy dreamed that she saw Aslan. Upon waking, she headed into the wood. Mistaking a rustling sound for Aslan, Lucy was disappointed to find Peter standing with his sword drawn. Before Lucy could ask Peter what he was doing, Caspian appeared and attacked Peter!

But with Narnians at his side, Lucy knew that the attacker could not be their enemy. Lucy called for the fighting to stop. Peter regarded his opponent.

"Prince Caspian?" Peter asked. "I believe you called?"

"Who are you?" Caspian asked. With that, Susan and Edmund came running into the forest.

The Narnians were happy to see their Kings and Queens of old standing before them.

Prince Caspian brought everyone back to his underground camp, where he and the Narnians had been preparing for battle. "It may not be what you're used to, but it's defensible," he said.

"What is this place?" Lucy asked as she stared at the drawings of herself and her siblings on the wall.

Caspian lit the torch to illuminate Aslan's Stone Table . . . they were standing inside Aslan's How!

The time had come to put Caspian on the throne, and the
Narnians were ready. King Peter and the Narnian war council
discussed how to attack Miraz's castle.

The Narnian army approached the castle in the middle of the night.
"For Narnia!" Peter called as he raised his sword and charged towards
the Telmarines.

Peter fought alongside the bravest Narnians: the Satyrs and Fauns. Together they charged ahead.

They battled the Telmarines as best they could, but in the end, the Telmarines forced them to retreat back to Aslan's How.

Peter knew it would take more than spirit to defeat these soldiers — they needed help. They needed Aslan. Peter sent Lucy deep into the forest to find him. The Great Lion quickly appeared before her.

Lucy threw her arms around Aslan, and then asked him why he hadn't come sooner to save them. "Things never happen the same way twice, dear one," he said. "I think your friends have slept long enough, don't you?"

And with that, Aslan woke up the sleeping trees, and headed towards the battle.

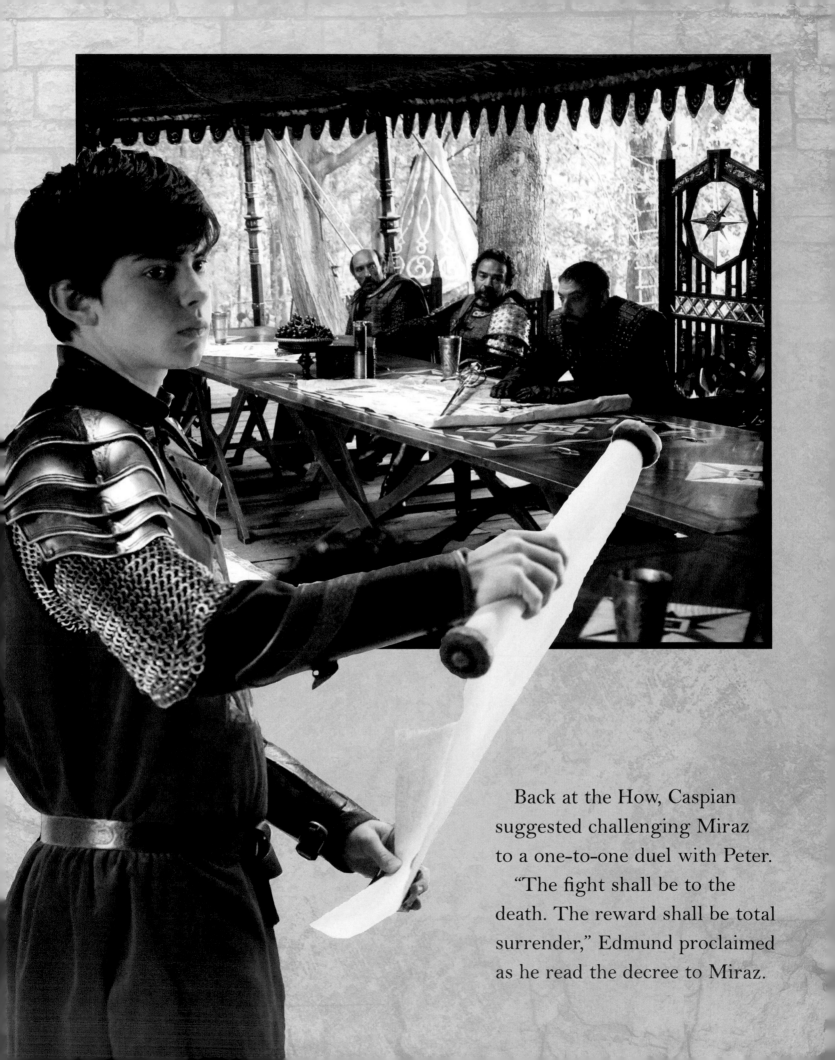

Back at the How, Caspian suggested challenging Miraz to a one-to-one duel with Peter. "The fight shall be to the death. The reward shall be total surrender," Edmund proclaimed as he read the decree to Miraz.

Miraz accepted Peter's challenge to a duel. Just as Peter had Miraz cornered, he handed his sword to Caspian, saying that it was not his fight to end.

"Keep your life, but I'm giving the Narnians
back their kingdom," Caspian said as he towered
over Miraz.

Even after Caspian defeated Miraz, the Telmarines continued to advance upon the Narnians with their swords drawn high.

"Narnians, charge!" bellowed Peter.

They braced themselves for the attack, but they were no match for the Telmarines. They needed something more. . . Just then, the trees launched their attack on the soldiers! Peter knew instantly that Lucy had found Aslan.

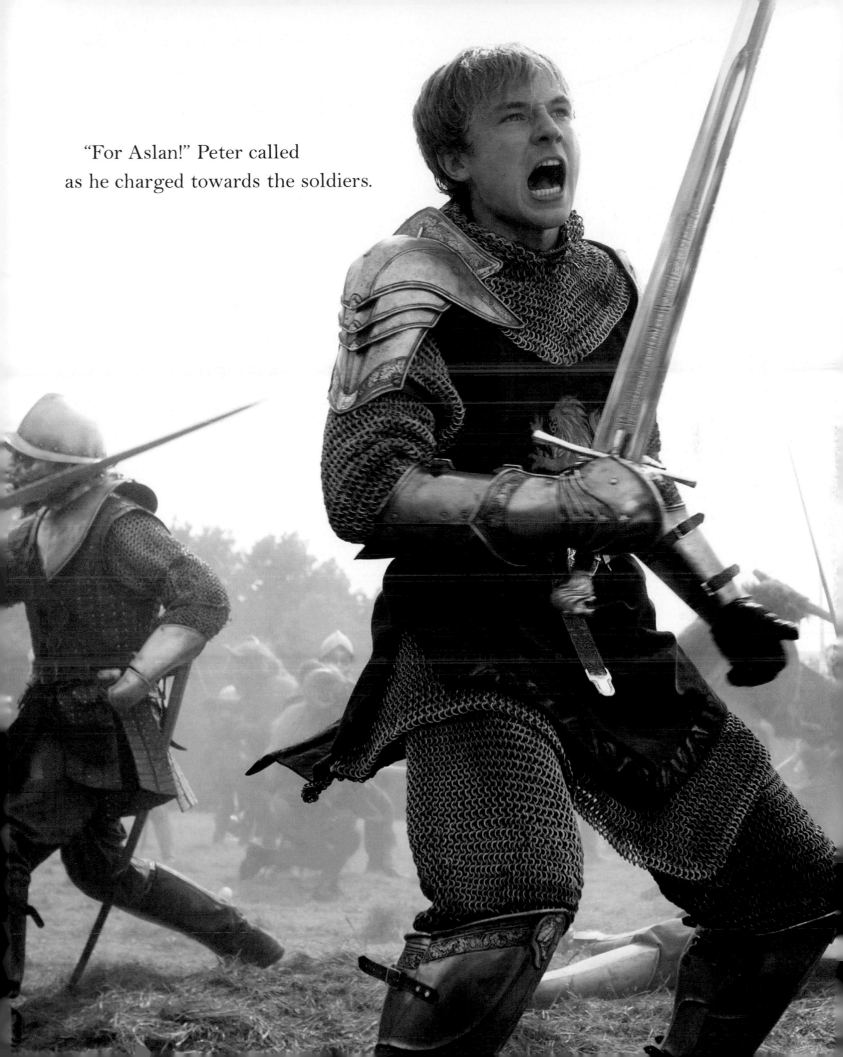

"For Aslan!" Peter called
as he charged towards the soldiers.

The Telmarines retreated towards the bridge that would lead them out of the wood and away from the Narnians. As the soldiers rushed ahead, Aslan appeared before them. He let out a mighty roar and defeated the soldiers once and for all.

Gathered before a crowd of Narnians, Peter and his siblings dropped to their knees, heads bowed before the mighty Lion.

"Rise, Kings and Queens of Narnia," Aslan said.

He declared Caspian the new King of Narnia, as Peter handed his sword to Caspian.

"I'll hold it until your return," Caspian responded, in awe of this great honour.

The Pevensies took one last look at their beloved, magical land, and then walked through the doorway that Aslan created in a nearby oak tree. On the other side of the doorway, the children found themselves back on the train platform in their school uniforms.

CORNELIUS' LESSONS

Cornelius teaches Caspian about the old ways of Narnia.
He tells the young Prince about the forest's Talking Beasts and
Mythological Creatures. The Narnian words listed below
can be found in the puzzle across, down and diagonally.

ASLAN	DRYAD	NYMPH
BEAVER	LAMPPOST	TREE
CENTAUR	MAGIC	WITCH

A X R O Q J K B D H E S V I T
J B I J H F U T O P L N H F J
D G L Y J S N I R S J Y D L P
R E P B T L E M T E C M N I W
Y H A C Z C V O A N E P T O A
A C S K W I T C H Q A H S U I
D W L R T O M I M G R F O W E
K H A Q E J C X J P T A I C Y
U E N U I C E S I K V C F Y X
A O L B L F N A C E Z T P M O
P C V F S O T Z H S A M R A H
L W S L E L A M P P O S T G S
D Y P G I M U S V N F E K I N
G B E A V E R N F S M B F C L
E V D I F D T B A Y O G W L D

SUSAN'S SCRAMBLE

Unscramble each of these words to spell
out a Narnia-themed word.
The first letter of each solved word, reading down,
spells out the answer to the question:

Who was the Dwarf that Lucy and Susan referred to as their Dear Little Friend?

_____ **MARINETEL**

_____ **EEEEPRIPHC**

_____ **DERNUGRUDNO**

_____ **ZAME**

_____ **TREEP**

_____ **NGIK**

_____ **OYRVI**

_____ **SERNURY**

LUCY LEADS THE WAY

Draw a line to help Lucy
lead the others to their allies.

START

FINISH

A MIGHTY PLEDGE

Reepicheep may be small, but his sword is swift.
Solve the maths problems below.
When you have solved them all, fit the letters
into the numbered spaces to reveal Reepicheep's promise.

I	=	10	-	2
U	=	12	+	11
W	=	9	+	2
L	=	8	÷	2
F	=	3	×	7
R	=	6	+	4
V	=	25	÷	5

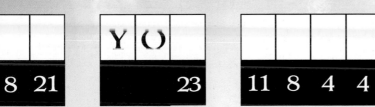

YO — 8 21 — 23

— 11 8 4 4 — EAD — 4 — S, 23

E — 11 — O E — 21 21 10 — YO — 23 — O — 23 10

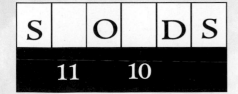

S O D S — 11 10

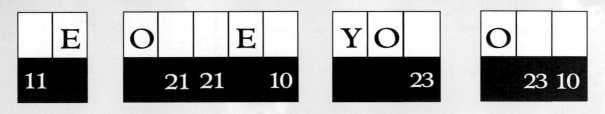

N ESE ED Y. — 23 10 10 5 4

HIDDEN DANGER

Lucy wakes up with a start. She and Peter hear a noise in the wood! Cross out the word ENEMY wherever it appears to reveal an important message for Peter.

PENEMYUTENEMYENEMYDOENEMYW
ENEMYNENEMYENEMYYOUENEMY
ENEMYRSWENEMYORENEMYDYE
NEMYENEMYOUENEMYAREENE
MYSUENEMYRROENEMYUNENE
MYDEDENEMYENEMYBYENEMY
CENEMYASENEMYPIENEMYAN
ENEMYSENEMYARENEMYMY
ENEMYENEMYENEMYENEMY.

PUT DOWN YOUR
SWORD YOU ARE.
SURROUNDED BY
CASPIAN'S,
ARMY.

HUNGRY FOR POWER

Glozelle and Lord Sopespian know that Lord Miraz is looking for war.
He will stop at nothing to defeat the Narnians.
Fill in the missing vowels A, E, I, O or U below to reveal Miraz's motive.

L_RD M_R_Z
W_NTS T_
ST_ _L TH_ THR_N_.

CROSSWORD

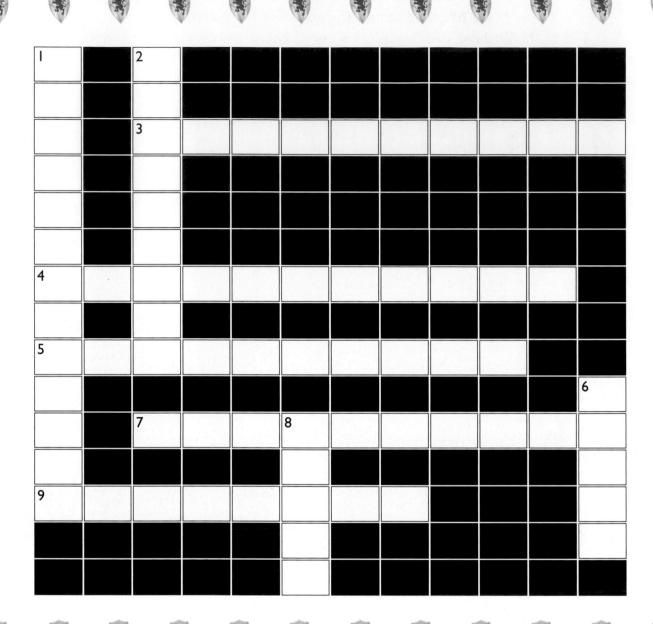

ACROSS

3. A helpful mouse
4. Where had the Pevensies lived in Narnia?
5. What was missing from the treasure chamber?
7. Who were the Narnians afraid of?
9. Which dwarf hurt Prince Caspian with his sword?

DOWN

1. Who attacked Peter in the forest?
2. Who was Prince Caspian's professor?
6. Who did Peter send Lucy to find?
8. Who wanted to steal the throne?

WORTH A THOUSAND WORDS

Look carefully at the image below.
When you are ready, turn the page and test
how well you remember what you have seen.

TRUE or FALSE

Without turning back the page,
answer the questions below from your memory.

1. Cornelius' left hand is resting on the table. □ True or False □

2. The arrow's feathers are coloured red. ■ True or False □

3. The arrow has landed in a map of Narnia. □ True or False □

4. Sand is running through the hour glass on Cornelius' desk. □ True or False □

5. Cornelius' gown has golden embroidery on the cuffs. □ True or False □

6. There is a skull on Cornelius' desk. □ True or False □

7. The curtain is red and gold. □ True or False □

8. Cornelius is wearing glasses. □ True or False □

9. The hour glass is smaller than the globe. □ True or False □

10. Cornelius is holding a magnifying glass. □ True or False □

HIS FATHER'S SON

Cornelius tells Caspian that Lord Miraz
is responsible for the death of Caspian's father.
Help Caspian find his way through Miraz's castle.
Follow the word BETRAYAL through the maze below.

START

B E K J K Y A L O Q S D
V T R A Z A H B P L G P
G C J Y O R J E T W H I
D B L A I T O I R M C O
U E I D B E P Y A E T G
M T U S L Q K A F B R A
W R O Y A M W L N L N Y
Y A G A P T E B W A C A
A X T R D R G I K Y W L
L B E K W A Y A M A
FINISH
P Q S U I D U L G R
O I W F M N S B E T

DESIRE TO BE KING

Narnia needs a new ruler.
Trace the line to connect the crown with Narnia's rightful ruler.

SHIELDED

You'll need a friend to play this game. Each player takes turns connecting the shields, one line at a time, to make a square. When you complete a square, put your initial in it and take another turn. You can use your opponent's lines to make a square. The player with the most complete squares wins!

WHO'S WHO?

Can you match each person to their name?
You have to unscramble them first!

a) PIECERHEPE

_____

b) LANAS

_____

c) TREPE

_____

d) SANUS

_____

e) NIPCASAINCERP

_____

f) RIZAM

_____

NOT ALL WILL RETURN

The Pevensies must return to England.
Not all of them will get to visit Narnia again. They must say goodbye.
Help the Pevensies find their way back to the train station.

START

FINISH

ANSWERS

Page 46. CORNELIUS' LESSONS

```
A X R O Q J K B D H E S V I T
J B I J H F U T O P L N H F J
D G L Y J S N I R S J Y M F P
R E P B T L E M T E C M P W A
Y H C Z C V O A N E N H T O I
A C S K W I T C H Q A H S U E
D W L R T O M I M G R F O W Y
K H A Q E J C X J P T A I C X
U E N U I C E S I K V C F Y H
A O L B L F N A C E Z T P M O
P C V F S O T Z H S A M R A H
L W S L E L A M P P O S T G S
D Y P G I M U S V N F E K I N
G B E A V E R N F S M B F C L
E V D I F D T B A Y O G W L D
```

Page 47. SUSAN'S SCRAMBLE

TELMARINE
REEPICHEEP
UNDERGROUND
MAZE
PETER
KING
IVORY
NURSERY

Answer: TRUMPKIN

Page 48. LUCY LEADS THE WAY

Page 49. A MIGHTY PLEDGE

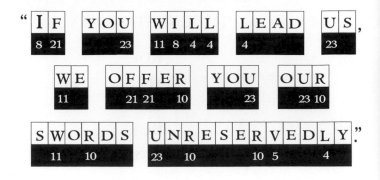

"IF YOU WILL LEAD US,
WE OFFER YOU OUR
SWORDS UNRESERVEDLY."

Page 50. HIDDEN DANGER

PUT DOWN YOUR SWORD.
YOU ARE SURROUNDED
BY CASPIAN'S ARMY.

Page 51. HUNGRY FOR POWER

LORD MIRAZ WANTS TO
STEAL THE THRONE.

Page 52. CROSSWORD

ANSWERS

Page 54. TRUE or FALSE

WORTH A THOUSAND WORDS

1.	FALSE	6.	TRUE
2.	TRUE	7.	FALSE
3.	FALSE	8.	FALSE
4.	FALSE	9.	TRUE
5.	TRUE	10.	FALSE

Page 55. HIS FATHER'S SON

Page 56. DESIRE TO BE KING

Page 58. WHO'S WHO?

a) REEPICHEEP

b) ASLAN

c) PETER

d) SUSAN

e) PRINCE CASPIAN

f) MIRAZ

Page 59. NOT ALL WILL RETURN

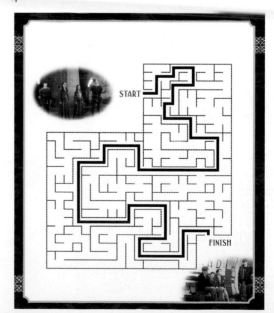

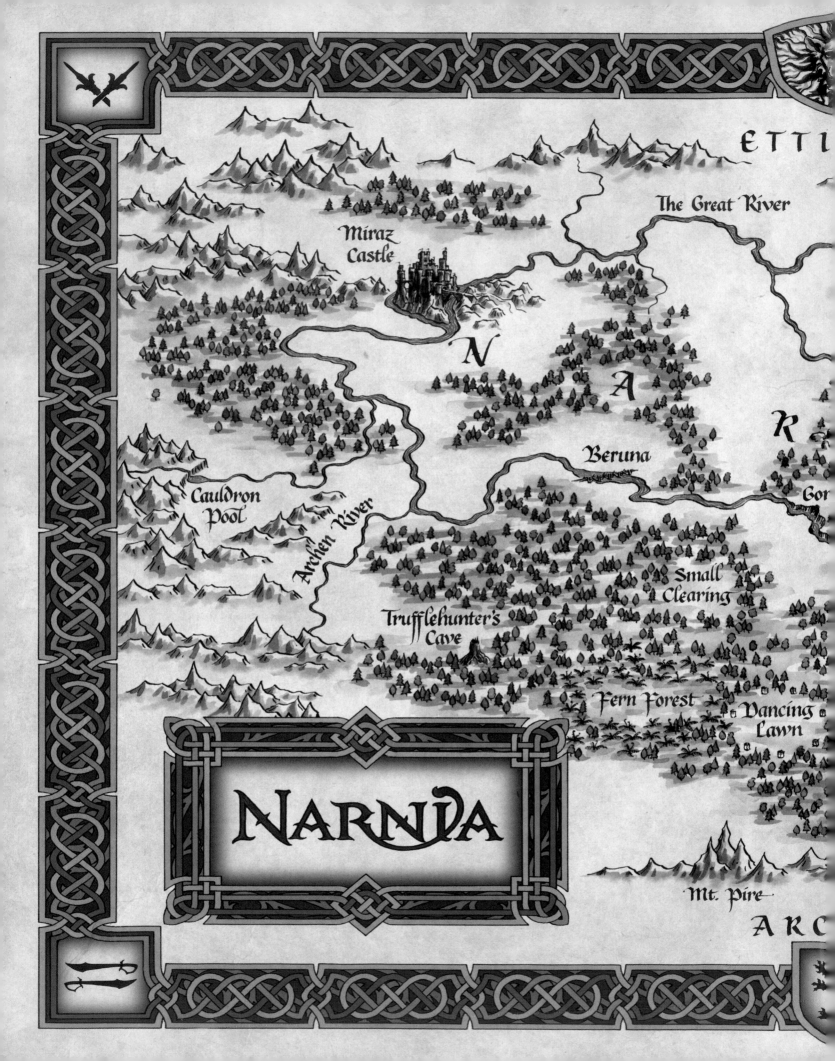

ETTI

The Great River

Miraz
Castle

N

A

R

Beruna

Gor

Cauldron
Pool

Archen River

Small
Clearing

Trufflehunter's
Cave

Fern Forest

Dancing
Lawn

NARNIA

Mt. Pire

ARC